Flower Boy

Nathan David Limon

To the Reader:

This is not meant to be easily digested. It is an endless love letter to those that cannot find the words to describe their endeavors. I hope you see these words and shed your pride and insecurities. Allow yourself to be human and feel everything you hide from the world. You are loved. We are all imperfect but that is what makes us capable of infinite possibilities.

Enjoy,

    -   N.D.L

Book I: Broken Promises

I. Blues:

Please listen to some of my melancholy blues.

The way I have learned to deal with all of my emotional hues.

My soul a sinking ship in overcast weather.

Filling all of the crevices, trying to get it all back together.

I have taken on too much water as I reach out towards the sky.

All I see are shades of blue as I gently close my eyes.

II. Fall:

My heart feels like it's falling through the cracks of
overwhelming sorrow.

Trying to reach down my own throat, squeeze it back to life
and survive until tomorrow.

Just like every day it seems, survive until tomorrow.

I have nothing left, ribs folding over a cavity that's
hollow.

My veins pumping poison to provide a numb sensation.

Too many thoughts of pain have filled my memory's rotation.

Trying to overlook the tick of anxiety's vibrations.

III. Memories:

I can't remember what she tastes like, but I can tell you nothing has ever been sweeter.

I can't remember what she smells like, but I can tell you that even the most beautiful flowers have become dull.

I can't remember what it feels like to have her skin against mine, but I can tell you I've never felt more at home.

I can't remember what it feels like to see her after long day, but I can tell you how even the slightest glimpse of her made me float.

I can't remember what it feels like to hear her voice say my name over and over, but I can tell you no other melody has made me melt.

I can't remember if I should still write this down, but I can tell you it's all I have of her.

IV. Cliché:

I'm a walking cliché.

Bad boy, broken heart, I'll come around someday.

Running around the garden I've created inside my head because I haven't found my way.

Here are the flowers that have grown from my scars, have a bouquet.

Slipping in and out of consciousness, my mother said it would be okay.

Find me in the darkest parts of my memories, I'll be gone, my spirit is on layaway.

V. Reflection:

Transparent surface reflecting my own image right back at me.

Sometimes it's glowing with optimism and sometimes my cold, rigid scars show.

I am myself, made up of the memories that have painted the canvas onto glass revealing my insides, while only exposing my outsides.

This painting runs skin deep, but only one pair of eyes can see what's truly underneath.

VI. Nostalgia:

Nostalgic tingles fill my gut.

Cocoons filled with memories crack open.
Butterflies seem to flutter around my throat and escape
from my mouth.

As if to say hello and goodbye in a matter of minutes.

To remind me that life is fleeting but it's all beautiful
with each passing day.

To never forget how I got here, but to keep pointing me in
the right direction.

VII. Flower Boy:

Soft, docile, and sweet.

I let others walk into my garden and do as they pleased.

All the while my garden was dying, and I couldn't find a way to keep it alive.

The rains came and drove everything out and nothing was left.

Until a soft hand placed a seed in my damaged garden.

A solitary tree began to grow, and the roots spread themselves out.

This time I would only let those that treated me with kindness to enter my garden.

That will make all the difference.

VIII. Burden:

A heart carries a heavy burden.

Taking on the task of protecting what you hold most dear.

Providing shelter from those that seek to fill your mind with false images and accusations.

Heartache is nothing short of the life force inside of you calling out for rest.

Only so much can your heartbeat to the sound of hammering drums before it feels like it's giving out.

Take care of yourself, close your eyes and let the world go dark as you heal.

IX. Numb:

Sitting between dysfunction and   zero sensation.

Trying to decide whether I miss the feeling of the
hurricane inside of my mind or this feeling of newfound
invincibility.

From one perspective to the next, as if the dials in my
mind have turned too far.

I never wanted to feel numb, I just wanted to feel like I
wasn't struggling to survive.

X. Shadows:

Sometimes I scare myself.

As I sift through my own thoughts.

I can't help but wonder where it all comes from.

As if the darkest parts of me have crawled out from my own shadow.

To remind me just how much wrong I've done.

XI. Capsize:

Lost in mental waves.

I try to wade through my own thoughts, but they keep pushing me under.

I've learned to hold my breath until my lungs start to give out.

Soon they'll take on water and I will capsize.

XII. Breathe:

I can feel my rib cage expanding with each breath that shoots out of my lungs.

I can see it escaping my shuddering lips as I fight to stay warm.

Maybe if I give into the shivering, I'll become numb to the world around me.

For some reason I don't want to be.

XIII. Note to Self:

This is a reminder that you are not hard to love.

Your voice is not too loud, and you are not too soft.

Remember that you deserve the world and nothing less.

I promise.

XIV. Finite:

Forever is a heavy word.

Lost in translation, we forget that we are not infinite.

Our souls will depart as they see fit.

XV: Warmth:

I've found a better meaning for the color blue.

It extends over and over past me and you.

Waves and skies are filled by its pigment.

Stuck between heaven and hell, almost indifferent.

Feeds the birds and the bees and is quite the favorite amongst the trees.

Shy in nature but can pop in an instant.

Reminding the soul and body to never grow distant.

XVI. Cleanse:

I find solace in the rain that pounds against my window.

It's as if it's telling me that all will be washed away,
and I can start anew.

Start fresh when the sky rolls into crystal blue waves.

XVII. Tick:

Swollen lips exchange sweet gifts with white noise from some flicks playing in the background.

Bodies melting on old leather soaking up heated memories that won't be forgotten.

Train tracks pounding into the earth from heavy carts rolling along but the noise isn't enough to interrupt anything.

Faded panting echoes through the walls in time with the clock ticks, faster and faster.

XVIII. In Bloom:

I have watched my scars feed the flowers growing in my rib cage.

They aren't so lovely to look at, but they remind me of the trials I have endured.

Reminders that through the pain, beauty takes its place.

Even in the darkest of depths, new life can grow and thrive.

XIX. Hope:

Hope isn't what you are looking for.

You are looking for answers to the questions that no one has.

You must look inside of yourself and realize that hope resides in your fingertips.

You have the ability to request it at any time and place.

You are in charge of the road that will be laid ahead.

Hope is all you need.

XX. Spectrum:

I always feel too much or too little.

I am extremely quiet or obnoxiously loud.

I can either be cold or overbearing with affection.

For me, there is no middle ground.

I have learned to be two opposite ends of the spectrum, and
that is how I choose to live

XXI. Lovely:

Come, sink your teeth into me.

I am soft so that can be executed with little to no effort.

You realize this as other girls have before.

"You aren't like any other boys I've dated".

As if my fangs and blood lust don't seem as apparent.

Eat me alive and watch me stumble to find words when I try to protect myself.

I forgot that I was only the nice, quiet boy with wounds so grotesque most people stay away.

My lion roar is a defense mechanism, heeding those that come near that I am the most broken.

But that is why I am kind, so that maybe someday someone will decide that I am enough without pouring acid upon my wounds to be more presentable.

Take me as I am, I don't have much kindness left.

XXII. Honey:

Sweet and succulent.

I remember my first taste of honey and how addicted I became.

I could never get enough and now you're somewhere else.

All I can do is dream about the honey that pressed against my lips.

All I can do is crave for the skin that fed my hunger.

XXIII. Slip:

Struggling, starving, narcissist with an ability to make my tongue twist.

please listen to the words that slip between my lips because I'm trying to tell you that happiness does exist, and for you not to give in to the negative outrage that shadows the bloody knuckles on your fists.

What I'm trying to say is your lovely bones make sense to me, and as far as I can tell people have thrown stones at you in an attempt to shell out their own anger and jealousy.

Most people sit so long in their own despair that they forget what it's like to see the beauty out there, but you must remember that there truly is beauty out there, because when I look at you I understand that there is, truly beauty out there.

XXIV. Roses:

There are many roses in the garden. However, one always stands out amongst the rest.

The one you dare not pick in fear of it wilting slowly before your eyes.

Beauty beyond measure, it sways in the crowd with silence.

No other will compare, no other will make you feel alive.

XXV. Yellow:

Trying to find the warmth inside of myself.

The feeling of the sun peaking against my bones.

I need to remember what that feels like.

The feeling of my body becoming part of the world for a fleeting moment.

As I close my eyes and bathe in the yellows and oranges.

It's the only way I'll be able to keep going.

XXVI. Crown:

To the fatherless boy, you are the man now.

The crown has been placed upon your head.

Built up rage and angst will inhale you as the skies turn red.

Bloody knuckles and tired bones will be a permanent reminder of the growing pains.

Blinded by hatred, your sore eyes will beg for days when there is no rain.

There will be those that stand by you, so you never have to conform.

Your scars will glisten in the light so wear them with pride.

The ache inside of your chest will continue to subside.

Instead, flowers will grow in and around your heart.

Your soul will find peace instead of tearing itself apart.

Come young one, and do not be afraid of the darkness inside of you.

It makes you who you are, and the light will eventually seep through.

XXVII. Insomnia:

Sleep has become a significant part of my daily routine.

Filling the long hours with my eyes shut, just to pass the time.

The bags under my pupils carry the weight of my struggles.

Honestly, I am just tired as all hell.

Hoping that maybe I'll wake up one day and feel my heart at peace.

XXVIII. BPM:

My heart seems to remind me of certain feelings I've felt before.

Rushing, racing, or silently thumping along to situations I find myself in over and over again.

I've learned to follow it more as the years go on rather than overthinking every moment.

It has taught me to be myself at all times because my mind can lead me to reckless abandon.

I've learned to trust the home I've created inside of my chest because it took so long to build myself.

XXIX. Moon:

I fell in love with the way she danced around in the dark.

Unafraid of the consequences that came with being out in
the night.

She stood tall like the moon, knowing that everyone who
looked at her would fall in love.

She knew the stars would beg for her kisses, but she fell
for me instead.

That is when I found out that love existed.

XXX. Shades of Brown:

Eyes like Mother Earth, dark in complexion but they hold the secrets to the universe.

Irises filled like a cup of coffee in the morning.

Gazes so strong, they wake up the soul of any one lucky enough to catch them ablaze in the sun.

Similar to fresh cocoa beans being harvested,

Sweet and with vigor, they view the world unbothered.

For these eyes are the color of soil, bringing life to all those needing help.

Only wishing to play a part, because they know things are better left unsaid.

XXXI. Strangers Again:

Once intertwined like laces, we've come undone.

Familiar face staring back at me, but I don't recognize the voice filling my ear drums.

I've felt this before, this overwhelming feeling of my heart getting heavy, my lungs gasping for air, and my body going numb.

Waltzing in and out of inconsistency.

You decided to leave again and now I am at the mercy of my own rotting dignity.

XXXII. Reality:

Come back down to earth, she said.

You're spending too much time in the clouds.

Listen when I tell you that you're just part of the crowd.

Your dreams might be too big so think a little less.

You might find that it is truly what's best.

XXXIII. Petals:

With winter comes the wilting of everything.

Our love felt like the flower petals as the season grew colder.

Falling away from where we started as pieces of us slowly hit the ground.

As if there was something missing from the once fiery passion.

Is this the beginning or the end of what feels like fatal attraction?

XXXIV. Voids:

Slipping continuously into a void that I've created for years.

Trying to dig myself out but I just keep piling everything on.

Hoping that from this darkness, I will bloom out into the light.

A rose surrounded by shadows can only concede to death.

That's what I've been told anyways.

XXXV. Lost Loves:

Flipping through photo albums always hits me with nostalgia.

Remembering the lips of those my heart once yearned for.

Memories flooding and taking me back to different pockets of time.

Reminiscing on lost loves and emotional flare ups.

It's easy to say I'm grown, and I'm fine.

Photographs just seem to make me pause and rewind.

XXXVI. She:

Even though the world makes me feel like I am nothing.

She makes me feel like I have everything.

XXXVII. Growing Pains:

Different walls have surrounded me every couple of years since I was a boy.

Wooden floors.

Different colored couches.

Fake mattresses.

My body has curled up on many of these with every new move.

However, I have only found comfort when your skin is pressed against mine.

XXXVIII. Insecurities:

They don't play too well with others.

Forcing me to make decisions based on fight or flight.

Trying to tell myself that I'm more than enough.

Acting like I have it all together when in reality I'm running from myself.

XXXIX. Withdrawals:

I never understood what it would mean to be away from you
until I started to notice myself falling apart.

I could feel my anxiety reach its peak over and over again.

I wonder if you ever feel it too, the kind of withdrawals
that give addicts the spins.

I know I feel it all the time, but I don't know if I'll
ever kick this feeling.

XL. First Love:

The one you never really forget.

The love you spend your whole life chasing after until you realize it's too late.

They've gone out into the world and you're left wondering what could've been.

XLI. Lone Wolf:

Red rivers flow from open wounds and internal battles are
never easily won.

Winning is always better than dying when the last breath is
yours.

The grim reaper even becomes afraid of the courage you
show.

The boundaries you break are the ones too difficult for
those that seek complacency.

Head down, always hungry for more, the world is forever at
your fingertips.

XLII. Metamorphosis:

Memories are engrained onto walls of pink matter.

Over time they become hazy as each blink captures stills of
our daily lives.

We always fight away the horrific moments like buzzing
flies.

We only seem to want to recount the heart fluttering
moments that feel like butterflies in our veins.

However, we must not forget that we aren't always the hero.

We must not forget the storms raging inside of us.

We are our light and dark times.

Every moment has allowed our hearts to continue to pulse
with life.

Reopen the gallery that is hidden to the world.

Become whole and feel the shadow winged moths fluttering
through your skin.

XLIII. Reminder:

You do not have to be a finished product to be loved.

You already are more than enough.

XLIV. To Whom It May Concern:

I'm watching you love someone else and I can't understand
how to feel at all.

I know I let you go but I guess I always wish I had one
more shot at it.

XLV. Wanted:

To be craved by another is a heavy burden on the soul.

Yelling out into the darkness hoping that they hear you is
a fool's errand.

The thing is they were never listening in the first place.

XLVI. Flower Girl

She always seemed to be fixated on the stars.

She always told me she was in love with the universe and
the way it displayed its beauty without trying.

I felt the same way about her.

XLVII. Freedom:

He whispered soft hymns to the world.

fields of green imprinted with his tracks.

His hands kissing the blues as they turned to pinks and
yellows.

Seeing only black, using his energy to find his way.

Sprinting into whatever may come next.

XLVIII. Gasping:

I've never had broken ribs before, but damn I swear there has been times where breathing becomes almost too painful.

My body only able to let out sorrowful whimpers.

Hoping that I can feel the ache subside and cry myself to sleep.

XLIX. Alive:

Feeling my heartbeat through my ear drums has always felt
so comfortable.

Whether it's drumming softly or racing to an unknown
location.

I think it's because when reality starts to crack and break
away
I can ground myself.

The loud murmurs forcing me to realize that I'm alive and I
have two feet planted firmly to the earth.

L. Good Enough:

MY BODY IS RIPPING AT THE SEAMS CONSTANTLY FIGHTING THESE
SHADOW FILLED NIGHTS IM FUCKING TRYING BUT ALL I CAN HEAR
IS THE SOUNDS OF DOUBT RINGING INSIDE OF MY EARS POUNDING
AWAY AT THE GLASS CAGE I'VE BUILT AROUND MY HEART UNTIL IT
SHATTERS AND MY EYES BREAK OPEN LIKE FLOOD GATES TRYING NOT
TO DROWN MYSELF IN MY OWN TEARS BUT DAMN IT SWIMMING
AGAINST THE CURRENT IS GETTING OVERWHELMING AND I CAN'T
HELP BUT FEEL LIKE I'M LOSING MYSELF MY OWN INSECURITIES
SPILLING FROM MY GUTS I JUST WANT TO BE GOOD ENOUGH I JUST
WANT TO BE GOOD ENOUGH.

Damn it someone just tell me I'm good enough.

LI. Aging:

Getting older means understanding that life is fleeting.

Nothing lasts forever and most things tend to be gone in the blink of an eye.

Hold on to the people you love, always.

LII. I Hate You:

"I love you, but I hate the person you are in this moment".

At least that is what I've come to understand from these three simple words.

Fucking over loved ones usually ends up with this phrase being reiterated.

I'm pretty damn used to it by now.

LIII. Coping:

I always push things to the back of my mind in hopes that they'll sit and rot.

Turns out the more I try to forget, the bigger the black hole becomes.

Swallowing the person I thought I was, and revealing the broken person I am.

LIV. Save Yourself, Kid.

No one is going to save you.

No one is going to go through the pain that makes you feel like the world is turning black.

No one is going to reach out into the void you reside in and pull you out with enough force to reverse the bullshit you've gone through.

Save yourself, kid.

Just remember to find the people that are willing to hold you through it all.

LV. Diet:

Breakfast: Scoop of anxiety and a cup of intrusive thoughts

Lunch: Existential dread mixed with stress from a job that you hate to make money so you can survive.

Dinner: Bowl of peace and quiet.

Keep it up for a while with meds.

You'll find life isn't so bad.

LVI. Smile:

Smile when the clouds don't let up.

When you feel like shit and it's hard to roll out of bed.

Even the toughest days seem to get easier when you let
yourself be happy.

LVII. Seeds:

Others planted seeds of doubt inside of my head.

I didn't realize that as I was growing, so were the damaging ideas that left me wondering who I was.

The roots spread inside of myself and turned me into what others wanted to be.

I became lost amongst a garden filled with thorns, but I craved the pain because it made me feel alive.

Now, I'm walking around and killing every notion and negative emotion that I have felt.

I am becoming myself again, and although I am exhausted, I will break free from these roots.

I will plant my own seeds of hope and bask in all the sunshine.

LVIII. Maybe:

I held your hand tighter knowing it would probably be the last time.

Our fingers danced nervously as we moved through the night.

I slowed my pace to see if I could make the moment last but that usually never works.

We stopped and turned towards each other for what I knew was certainly going to be the last time.

I pressed my hands against your face and leaned in for one more kiss.

Intertwined in each other, we faded away and let the world know that fate was always watching.

LIX. Let Go:

Letting go has to be the hardest part.

Where I realize that days keep passing and I'm not getting better.

I know why, but I can't seem to break my own heart.

I've done that enough already.

I guess it would be for my own good.

LX: Twinge:

Is it nostalgia, or emotions I've attempted to hide that causes the twinge in my heart when I see you?

I thought I boarded up and locked the doors where memories of you reside.

Turns out I never did a good job with that.

Turns out it's never been easy leaving the thought of you behind.

LXI. You:

I swear I don't want to love you anymore.

I don't want to look at old pictures and wish for you back.

I don't want to fight back the tears and emptiness I feel in my stomach knowing I'll never hear your voice again.

I just want to feel whole, but I'll never get that back either.

LXII. Ramblings I.

She asked if I wanted to lay my head on her chest. I could
never resist and climbed over to her. Our breathing started
to sync together, and I couldn't tell whose heart was
beating but I never felt more alive. She ran her hands
through my hair and the world started to melt away. Nothing
felt more right, nothing felt more safe. The sound of my
alarm broke through the void. My eyes shot open and I felt
the sun peeking through my window. Turns out I was just
dreaming about her again. My heart sank but I knew I had to
get up and start my day. I honestly couldn't wait for it to
be over so I could go back to that place. The only time I
get to see her is in my dreams. She's long gone now, and so
are the parts of me that left with her.

LXIII. Fix:

I am broken, but please don't try to pick up the pieces and rearrange them where you see fit.

Hold my hand and simply remember I'm a work in progress.

LXIV. Phases:

Parts of me have left with the kisses I've planted on others.

Nostalgia seems to flood my senses with memories.

I shut my eyes and remember details I thought I had forgotten.

Turns out love is never really lost.

It simply changes like the phases of the moon, sometimes it disappears but it always comes back to remind me of the light I once had.

LXV. Home:

Home is wherever my heart doesn't feel like erupting out my chest.

The bags under my eyes getting darker with no rest.

I know I'm getting better because the days don't feel as hard.

But damn I'm exhausted and scarred.

LXVI. Regret:

I feel my soul leave my lips as I try to figure out what to say to you.

I'm sorry that none of this is new but I'm trying to reach inside and make up for it too.

Stitch and sew my lungs back together, I think I've lost the air in my system.

My heart jumping and skipping to this melancholy rhythm.

I'm all in and I don't usually bet, I promise you I want to be more than a memory or regret.

LXVII. Sailing:

There is nothing like the feeling of my soul at ease.

Those moments where the world stops for a second and all is right.

As if the universe is saying, "Just hold on, you will make it. I promise."

LXVIII. Changes:

My mind still can't seem to comprehend the stillness in my head.

I almost think that this is too good to be true.

So, I'm just waiting to crumble and reshape my own reality again.

LXIX. Summertime Sadness

I always thought that when the sun shined for days on end I
was at my happiest.

Turns out I craved the summer because it meant I could run
away from everything that was pushing me closer to a
breakdown.

I could escape myself and have zero recollection of the
warm nights that broke against myself medicated nonsense.

At least I'll be prepared from now on.

No wonder I start to crave the cold days when my heart
falls to its lowest point.

LXX. Her:

If you see her, tell her she's all I have ever wanted.

Tell her I can't forget, and that I'm sorry.

I'm so fucking sorry.

LXXI. Ramblings II.

To feel alive is having someone's skin pressed against your
own. Getting tangled in each other's essence as time
becomes nonexistent. Lips and tongues intertwine and
breathing becomes a chore well worth the effort. Hips grind
against hips and everything becomes like instinct. Basking
in the heat of it all. Feeling alive is being tangled with
someone else, while the world knows nothing of the sort.

LXXII. Peachy:

Her skin reminded me of summertime.
Sunsets pressed against her body, hues of orange and pink
freckled the darkest parts of her.

Sweet to the taste always.

LXXIII. Best Friends:

We seemed to drift in and out of each other's lives.

Spending periods of time apart, only to give into the
curiosity that settled in every now and then.

I was still in love, and to this day I wonder if you ever
were.

Best friends no longer, lovers finally parted ways.

LXXIV. Embers:

Old love crackles like a dying fire.

Nostalgia seems to feed the embers glowing.

Turning back the clock and engulfing everything.

Remembering being burned over and over.

Holding onto the memories because I was scared of the dark.

I'm not so scared anymore, and I've got the charred parts
of my heart to prove it.

LXXV. Cracks:

You asked me to open my heart and you climbed inside.

You built a home inside of my chest and I furnished it to your liking.

I just wanted to be what you thought I could be, so our foundation was a bit rocky.

Until it all came collapsing down and I tried to pick up all the pieces and put it back together.

My hands were cut and bruised, and I was too tired to do it all alone.

So, it just so happens that our house was never really a home.

More like an escape from the broken realities we both hid from.

A shelter we both tried to keep upright so we could be okay.

Slowly but surely it all gave away.

LXXVII. Notice:

I want you to notice me.

Noting the scars, but instead of pulling them open, you kiss them gently.

Seeing me become emotional and providing reassurance.

Remind me what it's like to feel loved without worry.

Open my heart and I promise I will be yours forever.

LXXVIII. Torn:

I look back and wonder how we got here.

All the years and time spent together.

All the coming and going, hoping that we would somehow end up in the same place.

Now we have, except our paths have finally split into two.

Our fingers slowly unwrapping as we let go.

I never really got the chance to say goodbye but know that you made a man out of me.

I'll never forget you.

Especially when the roses bloom in springtime.

LXXIX. Songs:

It's strange how every song seems to remind me of you.

The bass settling in my ears sends vibrations to my chest.

Forcing my heart strings to play a melody similar to your voice.

I can't turn down the volume.

I can only hear the same song over and over again and hope I can drown out the noise.

LXXX: Past Loves:

To all who've held my heart in your hands.

I apologize for not being all there.

Most of the time I was in my head trying to decide if I was good enough.

Trying to break from my own demons but I simply let them run rampant.

I've broken my own heart more than once.

I'm learning to love again, and I hope you all are too.

LXXXI. 51/50

I think I was just tired of being angry.

My body was tired of holding in all of the hurt.

It decided to let me know and I probably should've listened
to the prior attempts it made.

I promise I'll listen to myself more often.

It's the only way I'll make it out of this alive.

LXXXII. Holding on:

I wonder how many times I've held myself back from feeling.

How many times I've decided to stay quiet and steady the shaking in my voice.

I lost touch with myself because I was told I wouldn't survive this way.

Turns out I'm still here, and that's all I need to know.

LXXXIII. Deserving:

I never really thought I deserved her.

The whispers from everyone around us grew to screams inside
of my head.

I left because they were getting too loud.

I didn't want to disappoint my own insecurities because
they
love when my heart aches.

LXXXIV. Always:

A sad soul wandering.

I was meant to take in the pain of others.

That is okay, but sometimes I feel ill.

Sometimes it is simply too much.

LXXXV. Caretaker:

Someone else may be holding you close.

I promised I would always take care of you.

I'll be here if you need me.

LXXXVI. Ache:

Tell me, when does it go away?

When does the image of you settle into the back of my mind?

I can't seem to leave you behind.

Please tell me, when does the ache go away?

LXXXVII. Pride:

I've never learned to swallow my pride.

I think it's because I refuse to vulnerable.

I refuse to let anyone in again.

~~So, stay the hell away from me~~.

Please come closer and let me be vulnerable again.

LXXXVIII. God:

I seemed to stop believing in a higher power for the longest time.

Until I peered into your eyes and seen the death of my ego and the rebirth of my soul.

LXXXIX. This Too, Shall Pass

This too shall pass.

The ashes from my charred heart will fall away.

I will look upon the field of blooming flowers created by
my sadness.

A bright, red rose bud blooming twice after it was snipped.

Settling behind the ivory fence inside my chest once again,
no longer begging to be quiet.

XC. Sigh:

I pressed my lips against your neck, and I could feel your heart beat faster.

You adjusted yourself and wrapped your legs around my waist.

My arms seemed to fit around you so perfectly.

There was nothing like the feeling of you.

Nothing like the feeling of melting away and forgetting what it was like to have my own soul as I fell into yours.

XCI. Reverse:

I don't know what to do.

I haven't felt this in a long time.

This is what I was afraid of.

I guess trying to run made it even easier to be caught.

Now I'm back at square one and I'm losing all of my senses.

Fuck this.

XCII. Fond:

Whenever someone asks about you, I always tell them you're probably doing okay.

I think it's easier to say that then to reach inside the memories I hold dear and try not to lose myself.

It always seems to be when I'm taking a step forward when something reminds me of you that sends me reeling.

I'm a recovering addict and you were my drug of choice.

XCIII. Naive:

I reconsidered us, knowing full well what had happened
before.

I hadn't heard the sound of your voice and part of me liked
it that way.

I missed you and there was no denying that.

So, I decided to try again.

I need to learn to not be so naive, but my heart seems to
think otherwise.

XCIV. Painkillers:

I'm always scared to feel numb.

I try to relax and remind myself that the meds are supposed
to be helping.

Maybe they are, maybe they aren't.

All I know is they are settling in and I can't feel a damn
thing anymore.

XCV. Forgiveness:

I'm no longer sorry for the lapses in judgment.

They have made me who I am.

I'm just sorry I haven't been kind enough to myself to let
it all go.

XCVI. Need:

Where do we go from here?

How do I get up every morning and go to sleep every night
without curling up and waiting for it to be over?

I need you.

How do I stop needing you?

XCVII. Learning:

I learned to love like my mother and ended up with a broken
heart.

So, I started to love like my father and that has brought
nothing but sorrow to everyone that has felt my touch.

Now I am learning to love like myself, and there has been
no sweeter release.

XCVIII. Hurt:

Please hurt me some more.

It's all that I know.

XCIX. 2 AM in California:

Mi amor.

The sun set hours ago, but the warmth of the world hasn't left.

You left me stranded here.

I won't be coming home.

I've found a new love underneath the stars.

C. Still Here:

I honestly didn't think I would make it this far.

I've given into my demons, and they've chewed me up and spit me out.

Teaching me that this battle is never really over.

I'm still alive and I've made friends with the voices that have told me to give in.

They need more help than I do, and I could always use some more companions.

Book II: Acceptance

CI. Self-Sabotage:

I think it's easier for me to say I didn't run away.

It's easier to say that I don't miss you.

I'm sprinting from my own self sabotage.

I like to think that I always do what is best for others.

This time I find myself wondering if I did the right thing
or if I tripped up on selfishness.

Am I what everyone thinks I am, or are these thoughts
simply a byproduct of my own undoing?

Was leaving you a heartless decision or was the fire inside
of you simply too strong for me to handle.

Does that make any sense?

I haven't made a whole lot of that these days but I'm
trying to give into these emotions that have welled up for
too long

Indecisiveness giving way to heartache.

Heartache I can physically feel, and it seems to be pulling
me farther and farther away.

CII. No Longer:

I don't want to be angry anymore.

I've spent too long hoping for apologies that I know I'll never get.

So here I am apologizing to myself for holding this all in.

For not giving myself a chance to breathe.

CIII. Love:

Love is not a predetermined destination.

It is the ultimate journey into the unknown.

It is seeing the best and worst of someone and providing shelter.

It is survival with a stranger turned everything.

It is melting into someone's soul and becoming one.

Love is and will always be the most powerful force in the entire universe.

What would you do for love?

CIV. Skeletons:

I've learned that we all have skeletons in our closets.

Some stacked higher than others.

If you knew what I was hiding, would you still think highly of me.

Probably not, so just walk away and set yourself free.

CV. Better:

Please help me become a better man.

Help me understand what it means to love again.

I ached for so long and I've hurt so many people.

Insecurities taking over, making my heart feeble.

I want to grow and be myself after all.

Before I find myself lost and I fall.

CVI. Tendencies:

Lucky boy with bad tendencies.

I promise it's not an invitation.

I am not here to have seeds planted behind my rib cage because the thorns will eventually prick my heart.

I just want to let it all grow out, even the weeds will flourish.

That way I can smile and say, "this is what has gotten me here and this is what will keep me going".

CVII. Emotions:

May someone understand my anger and realize it is just hurt.

Hurt from watching the world pass by the people I love because they have to struggle to survive.

Help keep me upright while I carry them all on my shoulders to somewhere safer than what they have experienced.

CVIII. Left:

I left and maybe everyone should know why.

Maybe everyone should know that it wasn't easy.

I walked away from a girl that I loved because I was going
through hell myself.

People will have their opinions and can continue to wonder.

All I know is that I'm trying to figure it all out.

I've been trying for so long.

CIX. Steps:

There are moments where I wonder if I even want to be here.

If all this effort will truly be worth it.

Then I am overcome by joy.

I've come so fucking far, why in the hell would I want to stop now?

CX. Narcissist

I don't mind the names anymore.

I guess it just shows how far I've come.

How I'm learning to grow out of my insecurities.

I'm not even close to being done yet.

CXI. Found:

I lost my voice trying to speak up for myself.

I was trying too hard to make certain people hear me.

Trying too hard to make them give a damn.

I'm finding my voice again and it doesn't sound like me.

A different kind of roar, one that refuses to back down.

I'm adjusting and I hope the whole world hears it.

CXII. Tried:

We were both broken.

Constantly trying to pick up the pieces left behind by others.

We rearranged them together but couldn't figure each other out.

We tried too hard, and I think that's why we never really fit together.

CXIII. Crave:

Our fingers fold in and out of each other.

Fighting every urge to let go.

We've finally run out of time.

It's time to let go, love.

It's been too long.

CXIV: Vulnerable:

I could go on and on.

Trying to count the ways I've loved and lost.

I haven't fully opened up to anyone in a long time.

I was once told being vulnerable is the key to human connection.

What if I told you vulnerability has torn me apart often with no remorse?

I don't want to go back to that place anymore.

CXV. Stuck:

You never really knew me at all.

Transfixed on an idea of who I am.

Instead of who I can become.

Or is it the other way around?

I'll never really know.

CXVI. Insomnia:

Created by this need to go over every decision I've ever made in my life.

Constantly asking what if or what could've been.

I should start asking myself why I take so long to accept things.

Maybe I'm just curious.

I have to learn to stop blinking and ending up with bloodshot eyes at 3 AM.

CXVII. Stoges:

I seem to crave cigarettes when I feel anxious.

You used to tell me to stop smoking because it was bad for me.

I usually crave things that are bad for me.

Or maybe it's just things that make me numb to the thoughts that have plagued me for so long.

CXVIII. Saved:

Old conversations saved.

I try not to go back and dissect them.

What I would've said and could've said.

I need to stop going back to what you said before because
it wouldn't be the same now.

I need your voice to go away.

CXIX. Faded:

Faded memories are my favorite.

The only times I can remember them is when I'm half past gone.

When I can't even remember my own name.

The pieces come back into place.

Drinking to remember, not to forget.

CXX. Fuck:

Fuck.

I can't seem to imagine myself placing my hands on anyone
else's hips.

I can't imagine my lips pressing against anyone else's.

My arms wrapped around you with your hands melting into my
back.

I'll find you in my dreams again.

CXXI. Favorite:

I know I'm still your favorite.

Or am I not?

Is my ego deceiving me again?

I can't tell, but I hope I'm still your favorite.

CXXII. Grow:

I have found myself in the darkest parts of my own soul.

Taking myself by the hand and heading into the light.

There is no sweeter feeling than climbing out of the hole so desperate to keep me encased in the shadows.

Every day is a blessing, and with each breath I am reminded of what it's like to be alive.

CXXIII. Frozen:

The harshest winters leave the world bitter.

A cycle of life and death.

When the days are the darkest that's when everything
strains a bit more.

The sun will come soon, don't give up yet.

CXXIV. Two:

I have to dig through myself to really understand why I am the way I am.

Some days I don't even recognize my own voice.

I try to believe I'm strong.

Most of the time I'm just building up my own walls higher and higher.

That way people won't see the weakest parts of me.

I don't know if I like it that way.

CXXV. 4 AM:

It's 4AM and I can't sleep but what's new.

I guess my body is adjusting.

This is around the time you would cling onto me because of the nightmares.

I'm sorry all I could do was hold you and tell you it was going to be okay.

I always wished I could do more.

CXXVI. Oxygen:

You are the air that I breathe.

Providing me with enough life to help me stand on my feet.

My lungs are suffocating now that you're away.

How did this happen?

How did you manage to get ahold of my heart and make me forget how to function properly?

I'm losing my senses and close to blacking out.

I guess this is what I get for not trying hard enough.

CXXVII. Fire:

She had a fire in her eyes that put the sun to shame.

The kind of burning that left an impression on me.

I can't forget those eyes.

Neither will I forget this suffocating feeling I have knowing she kept mine alive.

The fire in my eyes is gone and I can't seem to get it back.

It's all gone dark now.

CXXVIII. Reminder II:

You were created from out of thin air.

Stars exploding over and over again to create the atoms that make up who you are.

Remember that makes you magic.

Remember that you are one of a kind.

Head held high, don't forget to love yourself as much as the universe does.

CXXIX. M:

I can see life and death in her eyes.

The death of my pride, ego, and sadness.

The life I want to have, to take care of her.

She doesn't even have to try.

They say eyes are the windows to the soul.

Hers are the windows to my past, present, and future.

CXXX. 20/20:

A craving left unfulfilled will drive the most sane person blind.

Tunnel vision led by instinct leads to decisions unhindered by consequences.

Hindsight is always 20/20 but it doesn't matter when a need isn't met.

Consequences don't matter until it's too late.

CXXXI.(Drunk)Ramblings III.

I can reach inside my chest and reveal the truth about how
you make me feel and not turn different shades of red. How
I could write twenty different lines about your lips and
how they sit so perfectly on your face. How they perch so
softly like clouds on a summer's day. Your skin, my sun,
and remembering that my mother told me I could go blind if
I stared too long, but I stopped caring years ago. Your
eyes are my favorite kind of chocolate. The kind that
reminds me that the world is sweet and bitter at the same
time and to enjoy it all because it won't last long. Your
hair, the waves gently peaking, reminding me of my love for
the ocean and how it is full of secrets, but I want to know
all of them. Your voice, my favorite song, the kind I want
to put on repeat. Drunk poetry is the best poetry because I
never seemed to have the courage to say this to you in fear
that you wouldn't feel the same. You wouldn't feel the
fixation, the addiction, the adoration. Now all I'm left
with is memories that seem to cut so deep I can't pick up a
pen without it all being about you. It's all I have, please
let them know I need another drink so I can remember what
it's like to fall in love with the way you are so
effortlessly beautiful all over again.

CXXXII. Another:

I pressed my lips against someone else's

Relieved that I felt nothing.

Just enough to forget.

I guess that's all I needed.

A simple reminder that I'll be okay.

CXXXIII. Watch Over Me:

She always had a knack for keeping me safe.

She questions my motives and decisions.

Not to reprimand me but to help me find myself.

Always watching over my heart and soul.

Always my guardian angel.

CXXXIV. Trouble:

"You're trouble"

I think everyone I have ever met lets me know that.

I don't know what that is supposed to mean.

I don't know if I'm even trying to be bad anymore.

I promise I don't want to be trouble.

I guess I'm just better at seeking it out.

CXXXV. Mess:

IcantseemtounderstandwhyIevendothingsanymore.Imtryingtogras
pontomyownrealityanditsgettingharderwitheachpassingmoment.I
dontwanttokeepgoinglikethis.Idontwanttokeepmakingthesamemis
takesoverandoveragain.Ijustwantneverythingtobeokay.Ijustwan
ttofeellikemyeffortisworthsomething.

CXXXVI. Escape:

I've always found it easier to escape from the voices inside my head instead of actually dealing with them.

I still haven't found a way to stand up to them.

I haven't found a way to shut them out.

CXXXVII. Chasing:

I've learned to accept what he did to me.

Sometimes I can't help the world getting dark like it was before.

It wasn't my fault.

It wasn't the alcohol or the fear.

It wasn't my fucking fault and that's all I need to believe in.

Or was it?

CXXXVIII. Revelry:

It always starts with one.

Indulging until the world starts to blur.

I can feel the shift in my head.

The sadness is gone, for now.

CXXXIX. Cavities:

The sugar always keeps my mind afloat.

Feed me the overwhelming attention that I desire.

I stopped caring about my insides turning black a long time ago.

It's on the outside that matters most.

CXXXX. Drown:

I need reassurance.

Tell me that you need me.

Please tell me that you want me.

You could hold my head underwater but tell me what I want
to hear.

I will think you're trying to save me.

CXXXXI. Chances

Let me be better.

I know what I've done, and I've kicked myself so much that I can feel my mind turning black and blue.

Give me a chance to show you that I can be more than my mistakes.

CXXXXII. Plague:

Home is wherever I'm with you.

I grew up trying to mend everything that was out of my control.

My existence plagued by pain I didn't cause.

When I found you, all of the worries went away.

I finally found what I had been searching for.

A place to feel alive and comfortable in my own skin.

Thank you for giving me your heart and in exchange I gave you my soul.

CXXXXIII. Death:

My will to live is stronger than my want for death.

Most days I know I don't want to die.

I just want to not feel for a while.

CXXXXIV. Tomorrow:

"There is always tomorrow"

What if there is no tomorrow?

What if I blink and it's the last time I see it all?

How can I excuse the fact that I left it all up to chance?

I've stopped hoping for tomorrow because all I could have
is today.

CXXXXV. Right Through:

You see right through me.

I've tried so damn hard to hide myself from the world.

You see through the facade I put up so easily.

I wish you couldn't, then I wouldn't be forced to see
myself for what I truly am.

CXXXXVI. Vision:

Blurred vision.

It's all black now but I can feel the drops rolling down my cheeks.

I can't remember the last time I felt this way.

I've fallen so many times my hands and knees have permanent scuff marks.

I'm tired of falling.

CXXXXVII. Catch:

Feet don't fail me now.

If they do may you be there to catch me.

Hands wide open, please don't make me regret trusting again.

CXXXXVIII. Flow:

Closure doesn't exist.

Patch up your wounds.

Let go.

Don't look at them ever again.

I promise you don't want to bleed again.

CXXXXIX. Options:

I'm tired.

I just want to get lost with you.

I've decided that running away isn't my best option.

With you, it is my only option.

CL. Self-Care:

Realizing that the alcohol won't fix the sadness.

The sex won't fill the hole in my chest but rather make it larger.

The cigarettes will numb my soul but force me to look deeper within myself.

Self-care, not indulging in my own shitty tendencies to destroy myself.

Rather looking at all my bad and telling myself that I am good enough as I am.

I told myself I don't have to hurt anymore.

I don't have to run away from the pain.

CLI. Stop & Stare:

Maybe I would hate myself a little less if we never met.

I wouldn't try to make up for all the lost time.

I wouldn't stare in the mirror and pick myself apart.

It's been so long, but I've never been able to shake this feeling of doubt.

I've never been able to heal.

So, tell me why I always feel bad?

CLII. Erased:

I wonder if you've erased me from your mind.

I still think of the hypotheticals.

How easy it is for the world to remind me about you when you were in my life for so long.

That's all I'll have from now on, faint tugs on my heart strings played by the part of you that never left my soul.

CLIII. Losing Touch:

I seem to be losing touch.

Most days it feels like I'm dreaming.

I keep waiting for something to happen.

This is just how it's going to be from now on.

Floating along as time drags on.

Watching the world pass me by.

CLIV. Rough:

Do not be so rough with yourself.

Others have done the same and that's what you've learned love should be.

Be gentle with yourself and find that love is not a stampede on your soul.

Rather it is the rain brushing against your skin.

CLV. Tense:

I have to constantly remind myself to not be so angry at this world.

Unclenching my fists and loosening my jaw.

I forget how tense I've been for so long.

Like the ocean coming to a standstill, I can finally rest.

CLVI. Present:

Sometimes I get so trapped in my head that I forget that
there's a world waiting for me.

Waiting for me to stop and remember that it's not all bad.

Stop and smell the roses while you can.

You're still here.

Don't waste a breath.

CLVII. Moving On:

A red string of fate is stretching far too thin.

We only seem to be moving farther and farther away.

It's time to let go.

It's going to hurt, but we can't wait any longer.

Cutting ties once again.

CLVIII. Lift Off:

I stopped believing in myself and fell into a black hole.

I saw no way out and gave up.

Where there is no hope, there is no reason to live.

I thought it was all over until I looked up and seen the glimmer of the stars.

They seemed brighter than ever before.

When you hit rock bottom, just remember to look up.

The world will remind you that there is always a way out of the dark.

CLIX. Inspiration:

She was my muse.

I was in constant wonder.

Wishing to create a world where it was always perfect for her.

She left and my inspiration was gone.

My painting left unfinished while I drowned myself in my sorrows.

I can't seem to find any motivation.

She is gone, and with her my glowing palette has turned black and white.

CLX. Show Off:

I know I've come a long way from the desperation I once felt.

I've burned all of the bridges that were unkempt.

I didn't realize that would leave me feeling so alone.

Nothing to show off, nothing to fill my ego.

I always wonder if I should go back and rebuild those bridges.

I shouldn't.

There are better days ahead, and I never want to feel controlled again.

CLXI. Loved:

We shared love but only in passing.

We were never meant to be, but it was real while it lasted.

I think we both knew that it was destined to end like this.

Love in our past, no longer our present.

CLXII. Exhausted:

I'm starting to sink back into the void again.

I have to look down at my hands to make sure I'm not asleep.

Lucid dreaming leaves me wondering what is real and what isn't.

I hate this feeling.

Someone remind me what it's like to feel real again.

CLXIII. **GOOD**(bad):

I wonder if it was all worth it.

I'm still here.

I no longer need a prescription.

Does everyone else feel this numb?

So many questions that I'll never know that answers to.

Maybe it's better if I just stop asking questions.

Most of us know what happens to those who are too curious.

CLXIV. God:

I speak to the universe every now and then.

It replies with things that I don't understand.

Some days I beg and plead for forgiveness.

Other days I ramble about sweet nothings.

I just hope someone or something is listening.

CLXV. Restart:

Time to start all over again.

I can feel my heart racing and my thoughts snowballing.

Escaping from comfort is never easy.

It is the only way I will be able to find myself again.

I loved you, but it is time to love myself.

CLXVI. Disengage:

Always appreciate those who have left a significant mark on your life.

Never wish unhappiness on them.

You will spend your whole life hoping they suffer without you.

When in reality, you are suffering without them.

Do not bleed yourself dry ever again.

CLXVII. Someday:

I'm not suicidal anymore.

At least that is what I like to tell myself.

I somehow get lost in the same scenarios over and over again.

I have to ride the waves of sadness.

I know it will pass, someday.

CLXVIII. Sailing:

Prepare for the worst.

Hope for the best.

Nothing in this life is guaranteed.

Enjoy your highs and lows.

Accept that it is impossible to demand perfection and it will all be okay.

CLXIX. Lust:

I have butterflies all over again.

Fluttering with a lust for life.

The cobwebs are falling away.

I want to be alive; I missed this feeling.

CLXX. Non-Apologetic:

I seem to always want to apologize for my emotions.

Then I remember the ocean does not apologize for her ebbs and flows.

She simply exists.

CLXXI. Stop:

Close your eyes.

Feel the world around you.

Do not forget to live, instead of hoping you will catch your breath.

CLXXII. Everything:

I had it all.

I was too stubborn to realize that.

CLXXIII. Spins:

My head is spinning.

The world around me full of blurry faces.

I rub my eyes over and over again to refocus.

Something won't let me give up

I'll sit down here in the dark for a while and try again soon.

Wouldn't be the first time.

CLXXIV. Settle:

Why can't we settle down?

Why can't we keep our feet firmly on the ground?

We were never meant to stand still.

We were born to find each other and yet we are still lost.

CLXXV. Last:

I didn't get to tell you I loved you one last time.

I didn't think it would be the last time.

I try to hear your voice in the back of my head, but it seems to be fading away.

Reality won't ever settle in and I'll be chasing your ghost for the rest of my life.

CLXXVI. Forbidden:

She was forbidden fruit.

Everyone only bothered to stare in passing.

I couldn't help but reach out and pick her out of the brush.

Life hasn't been the same since.

CLXXVII. Sun Kissed:

The warmth kissed my skin.

A gentle gift after the storm.

I wonder everyday if I'm still supposed to be here.

It's all about the little things.

CLXXVIII. Letdown:

I've felt my heart sink faster than pouring rain.

Settling in my stomach, an anchor to the words that can't seem to find their way out.

A silent yell out into the world.

Another letdown.

I should always know better.

CLXXIX. Ocean's Apart:

Godspeed.

She turned and walked away.

I watched the colors fade into nothing.

I saw everything melt into the void.

I felt my soul chase after her.

Leaving me in the same place I've been since she left.

How I wish for the lights to come back on.

CLXXX. Fin:

There are no endings.

Simply new beginnings.

CPSIA information can be obtained
at www.ICGtesting.com
Printed in the USA
LVHW031019041119
636247LV00001B/393/P